Fairy Tails and Bedtime Stories for Children

How to Make Toddlers Fall Asleep Fast and Dream all the Night

Written By

Margaret Milne

Table of Contents

UNDERSTANDING IS KEY

The family of Oswald's lived in the beautiful city of Perth, Australia. This was a family of six, as Mum and Dad lived with their parents as well. Ryan and Mia enjoyed being spoiled by both their parents and their grandparents. And due to the luxury of having elders present at home, both Mum and Dad could work full time without the worry of a nanny or the children not eating well.

Mr. and Mrs. Oswald would wake up early in the morning. Dad would make breakfast which would usually be an assortment of chocolate chip and blueberry pancakes with fresh juice or even strawberry smoothies on Friday. Mum would make sure that both the kids were up and ready. Mum took care of all the little things; the uniform must always be free of wrinkles, and the hair must not be out of place. Thus, Mia takes after her mother, her books had no turned corners or dog eared pages. At the end of a school year, her books always looked as good as new.

This was a family that catered to the strengths of each other. If Mia was good at languages, Ryan was technical, he loved math and science. More importantly, he loved the science experiments, he loved the concept of elements complimenting or clashing with each other. It fascinated him.

Mia, on the other hand, was intrigued by people and conversations. She wanted to know their story, she wanted to help, listen, and laugh with them. The striking differences between two people living in the same environment and culture, yet having different opinions tickled Mia's brain.

Dad was an engineer, he signed contracts with billionaire companies and firms. Mum, on the other hand, was an architect, hence the perfection and sophistication. She designed and laid out plans for beautiful modern buildings as well to preserve the older historical models. You see, she did not just believe in building and creating new structures, she always believed in protecting and preserving the past. She would say that building and figures tell stories of a different time and a different life. They reflect both. The designer and the creator, and if you pay close attention to it, it might just fill you in about his tale. That was why she loved old monuments, it was because she loved their story. The hands that mapped it, and the hands that shaped it, she loved them all.

Their grandparents were big on taking walks. They took walks at 7 am and another at 9 pm before they went to bed. Grandma would bake whatever the children desired, the children loved her baked potatoes with tomatoes and onions. It was the perfect combination of tangy and filling as the children liked. They loved the tender chicken, and the crunch of the onion.

Ryan loved to help her out in the kitchen. He loved to run around in the kitchen, popping out pans and mixing and rolling. It was always a treat when the two would make noises in the pantry.

Grandpa and Mia loved to read. Grandpa would point out articles in the daily newspaper and in subscribed magazines that he thought Mia would enjoy or simply should read to increase her knowledge. Usually, Mia loved to read them all and would find them rather intriguing, yet occasionally, an article would bore her to sleep, and then, Grandpa would laugh at the young girl.

It soon became clear to them that Ryan wanted to become an engineer, and Mia wanted to become a psychologist. So Mum and Dad decided to plan accordingly. They chose for their children the best tutors, the best schools, and they started saving up. They told their children to plan their lives, the grades they needed to have to make it into the schools that they had chosen for them. As the children prepped for their studies and their preferred schools, so did their parents. They put aside certain amounts of money in a savings count, so they wouldn't have to worry about their tuition fees when the time came for their admissions.

It was how the family functioned, they worked together, aiding, and guiding each other. They were a team. Life went on and time passed. Ryan and Mia worked hard, and they received the acceptance letters as planned. There was a wave of celebration and cheers in the air. Grandma and Mom shed tears of happiness. It was as if all their dreams and hopes were coming true. There was a flair of love and happiness that surrounded the family.

Maybe, it was because the goodbyes were too near. The family who had always stuck together as a single unit, as a team, and as one. They were now supposed to say their goodbyes, stepping into a different life and start a new in a new place.

Ryan was moving to a different city in Australia for his university, and Mia was moving to the other side of the globe, to the USA, to study her degree in psychology. It was a few long months of planning, prepping, and a lot of shopping. They bought all the essentials to take with them, weather-appropriate clothing, and storage boxes in case of low cupboard spaces.

Grandma taught and blessed them with a few of her notorious and healthy recipes. Grandpa bestowed upon them the knowledge and red flags to look out for. Their parents answered every query and went over any situation that the two might find themselves in.

After tearful goodbyes and a long year of daily video conferences, a quick five-minute phone call just to ask the substitute of cardamom or a quick approval to check if the outfit they had on made them look cute or not.

Alas! The year passed, and it was time for the children to return home for their semester break. And so, they did.

Mia was full of stories of new adventures, friends, and experiences. She had so much to say about the case studies she had worked on in school, and just how fascinating they all were. Mia showed the family countless photographs of the day trips she had taken, solo and with her friends, of cooking disasters and successes. It was very clear that Mia was happy with her decision and was living the life that was meant for her.

However, Ryan was quiet. He didn't talk much or even laugh. It was as if he was lost in a world of his own or something was bothering him greatly. He kept well into his room only coming out for meals or when called upon.

That made their parents very worried indeed. They were concerned for their son and wished to help him, but they couldn't figure out the problem that was bothering their son. Ryan was just quiet, and he wouldn't share his worries with the family.

Until one day.

He came out to the dinner table and waited for everyone to be seated. Then Ryan cleared his throat rather loudly.

"I have something to say."

"What is it, my child?" asked an anxious Grandma, while everyone looked thankful that Ryan was finally ready to talk about what was bothering him.

"There is no easy way for me to say this because I know we talked about this earlier, and it was my decision entirely, but I can't do it anymore. I can't pursue engineering as a career." He said.

"I don't understand," said Dad looking worried.

"It's just not my passion, Dad. And I know you saved a lot to send me to a proper university, but it doesn't excite me, studying it doesn't make me happy." Ryan said.

"So, you want to leave your degree just because it's not your passion?" asked Grandpa, trying to clear out the problem. Ryan was looking quite angry in a way no one had seen him in a long time.

"Yes, it doesn't make me happy."

"Career and education are meant to give you a stable life and future, no one said the process would be easy." Said Grandpa quite sternly.

The rest simply looked worried and sad at what was going on.

"Well, I might just drop out, because I can't do this anymore," Ryan said and left the table.

Mia looked at her parents and said, "If it doesn't make him happy, he shouldn't have to do it, you know." Before leaving the table as well.

"Honestly, what're these children going off about? Careers aren't a walk in the park, they're hard work!" said Grandpa loudly, looking around and expecting the rest to agree.

"Dad..." Mum said, "You're right, careers are hard work, But I don't think that Ryan should make a decision he doesn't like because he's the one who's going to live with it for the rest of his life."

"She's right. And besides, right now he has the time to start over with something he enjoys, later he won't have the luxury of time." Dad added.

"And besides, you were so worried about him being so quiet, wouldn't you prefer that he studies something he loves, so he loves his life too? I know you just want him to be happy, let him choose what makes him happy," said Grandma softly, stroking her husband's hand.

For a minute, Grandpa looked confused. He seemed shocked, but soon, the gravity of the situation fell on him, and he nodded. Without a word, he got up and made his way to Ryan's room. He knocked and asked if he may enter. Ryan looked surprised but nodded.

Grandpa went and sat on the edge of his bed.

"So what is your passion?"

Ryan frowned, hesitating before he spoke, but then, "Cooking. I want to learn and become a certified chef."

Grandpa smiled and said, "You always did enjoy spending all that time with your Grandma in the kitchen."

"I did."

"Well, then, if that's what you want, son, I won't stand in your way. You have my blessing, and be sure to remember that I'm expecting a six-course meal of pure perfection when you've finished your journey," Grandpa smiled at him fondly.

Tears filled in Ryan's eyes as he lunged forward to hug the old man and thank him over and over again.

"Son, at times we forget that we need to understand first rather than preach, I just hope you always know that I will stand by you and that I love you."

"I love you too, Grandpa, and I know."

Everything was back to normal. Ryan looked forward to his new journey to become a renowned chef. Whereas, on the other hand, Mia continued her studies for becoming a famous psychologist.

THE TWIN SISTERS

Jessica and Isabelle were twin sisters with auburn hair and beautiful green eyes. They both had the same upturned noses and an identical mole on their left cheek.

The only difference between them was that Jessica had a birthmark, the shape of an upturned vase, on her left shoulder, while her sister didn't.

As beautiful as the two sisters were, they both had very ugly hearts. They would always steal toffees from their teacher, Mrs. May's desk, and every day, they would take the biggest apple from the fruit basket on the dining table. They would even refuse to share their lunch with their school friends!

One particular Sunday evening, the twins decided to camp in their backyard. They took out the camping kit which they had gotten on their eighth birthday and began to build it up. It was a beautiful day outside. The sun was shining brightly, and the leaves were changing their colors, now that autumn had arrived. The scent of freshly watered soil lingered in the air, and the birds chirped merrily from the trees. It was the perfect day for camping!

They drilled four holes in the ground and stuck in four pieces of logs. Then, they hammered in all the nails as instructed in the box.

They asked their mother for help to drape the cloth over the wooden structure. After that was done, Isabella ran inside her room to grab the fairy lights her mother had bought her. She draped it all around the tent, making it look magical. They placed an old rug and some cushions to bring some color inside the tent. Jessica even brought some marshmallows that they could munch on. The last thing that was left to do was to bring their camping kit.

It was a small box that they took with them whenever they went camping with their father. It consisted of a small pocketknife, some safety pins, a flashlight, and a spare rope.

Their little dog, Timmy, jumped around them in excitement, knowing that he would get to enjoy the tent that the twins were building.

He was a beautiful golden spaniel, whose fur always gleamed in the sunlight. He had a shaggy tail that never seemed to stop wagging. Right now, he barked with glee as his tail wagged more than usual. He had spotted the marshmallows!

"Getaway, Timmy. Don't munch on those marshmallows! They are not for you," said Jessica rudely.

"Urgh, he's just so annoying," added Isabelle. "Let me go lock him up in our room. At least he won't bother us then," she huffed.

Timmy whined as if he knew he was about to be locked up. But Isabelle still locked him in the room so that they would not be disturbed while making the tent.

A light chilly wind whipped their hair around, while the sun warmed up the inside of the tent. The two sisters sat inside the tent, telling each other ghost stories when a sudden idea struck Jessica.

"Let's bake vanilla cupcakes!" she shrieked. "They will be perfect in this weather!"

"Yes! And we can make pumpkin latte to accompany them!" Isabelle added.

And so, the twins ran to the kitchen, asking their mother to give them her secret recipe book. It had been passed down to her from generations, and it contained the best recipes ever.

"Can we please have it? Please mommy," pleaded Isabelle.

"It is a very special book, my child. I don't want you ruining it," said their mom, shaking her head.

"But mommy, we promise we will be careful," said Jessica, blinking her eyes up at her.

Their mother heaved a deep sigh, looking down at them sternly. "Well, alright..." she said. "But if I see even one page torn, you both will be grounded for a week, got it?

"Okay, mommy!"

"Thank you, mom! You are the best!"

"Be careful you two! I am going shopping. I don't want to see any mess when I come back, and you both need to feed Timmy, understood?" Their mother said sternly.

"Yes, mommy!" the twins said in unison.

And with that, the twins grabbed their mother's recipe book and opened up the page to the vanilla cupcake recipe.

"Flour... butter... eggs... milk... sugar," Jessica mumbled out the ingredients while Isabella collected them from the pantry. Isabella gathered the baking utensils and placed them on the counter, beginning to measure out the ingredients.

By the time they had made the batter, the kitchen was very messy. Both of them had flour plastered on their faces while their aprons were stained with the various ingredients.

However, they poured the batter into the cupcake tins and placed them in the oven. Soon, the whole house smelled of vanilla. Once they took them out, they decorated them with sprinkles and left them to cool on the counter.

Suddenly, there was a knock on the door, and Isabelle ran to the window to see who it was.

"Oh no!" She exclaimed. "It's Auntie Margaret! Quick, we should hide the cupcakes!"

"You're right! She will finish most of them. I will distract her while you go hide them in the tent, Okay?" said Jessica, taking off her apron.

"Okay!"

Jessica went to greet her aunt at the door, and Isabelle snuck out to the backyard to hide the cupcakes in the tent.

"Isabelle, my child! How are you?" said auntie Margaret, once Isabella returned from hiding the cupcakes.

"I'm good, auntie," said Isabelle, putting on a fake smile.

Their aunt stayed for over an hour, all the while the sisters kept thinking about the delicious cupcakes waiting for them in the tent. After what seemed like an hour, their aunt finally walked out of the door, waving a very cheery goodbye to them.

"Finally! I thought she would never leave," groaned out Jessica, rubbing her eyes and yawning audibly.

"At least now we can finally eat the cupcakes. I'm starving," said Isabelle.

"The last one to reach the tent is a rotten egg!" screamed out Jessica as she ran out the back door.

"Hey! Wait for me," Isabelle said, laughing. She ran after Jessica into the chilly autumn air. By now, the sun was descending into the horizon, casting beautiful hues of pink and gold across the sky. The birds were chirping in the trees, and a lone squirrel was flitting about in the backyard, munching on something.

"Isabelle! Something very bad has happened!" cried Jessica out in front of the tent.

"What?" said her twin, running into the tent to see what was wrong. "Oh no!" She said, looking down in horror at the disaster that had taken place.

The cupcakes had been placed in a corner of the tent on top of their camping kit. Most of them were missing, and the remaining were all covered with giant black ants! Right before their eyes, the twin sisters saw their cupcakes being taken away piece by piece.

"How could this happen? Why didn't you cover them with something?" said Jessica, her eyes filled with tears.

"I didn't realize this would happen!" cried out Isabelle. "It would've been better if we had just shared them with Auntie Margaret. At least we could've had a few of them.

"Do you think we have time to make another batch before mom comes home?" asked Jessica. But, she got the answer the very next moment when they heard their mother's car pull up in the garage. They gave each other sad looks before something dawned on to Jessica. "Oh no!" She cried, shaking her head, and slumping down on the ground.

"What now?" said Jessica, already annoyed that she didn't get to eat any cupcakes.

"We forgot to feed Timmy. And we didn't even clean up the mess we made in the kitchen! Mom is going to scold us so much!" cried Isabelle.

Jessica groaned, hopelessness washing through her. It was going to be a long night. And what's more, they were going to be grounded for sure!

BELIEVING IN YOURSELF

The toast on my plate waited to be buttered as I tried to get the knife from the cutlery stand. "You should have asked," interrupted mom, grabbing the knife for me. I smiled foolishly, opening the container. I picked the knife up and slowly swiped it over the butter bar, leaving the tracks behind. "Your bus will be here any minute," mom interrupted again. I left the other area unexplored and moved the knife back to my toast with whatever glory was gathered. My generosity was appreciated as I shared the loot equally to four corners of my toast.

I placed the knife back, grabbed the toast, and walked over to the door. "Your dad will pick you up, don't take the bus," mom instructed. I nodded as I enjoyed the few remaining bites. Suddenly, the school bus honked. I hastily filled my mouth with toast, grabbed the bag from the shelf, and left the house, saying goodbye to mom in the mouthful, weirdest voice. Before getting on the bus, I gave a quick look over my uniform to ensure that it was neat and clean.

The driver watched me going through the aisle and waited until I sat somewhere. I wasn't sure where to sit, so I walked to the end seats and sat beside Jacob. The bus driver pushed the button, and the door got locked up. It was rolling time!

"Where have you been?" asked Jacob, finding a way to start a communication. "Nowhere," I replied, staring outside the window. "I mean you were not in school for the past week, is everything alright?" Jacob asked, hoping for a proper explanation, but I wasn't in the mood as it takes me time to set back to school routines. "Just went over to my Grandma's place, nothing much." Jacob sighed and nodded.

My school was almost ten minutes' drive away from home, and my location was the last in the bus's route, so the bus driver always picked me up in the end which was a benefit for me since I didn't have to wake up early in the morning. I could walk to school too, but my mom is overly possessive and thinks that it isn't safe. As time flew, we reached our destination.

The bus honked, and the school gates were opened by the guards. In no time. We were off the bus. I checked my wrist-watch, and there was still a half-hour remaining in class. I looked around, searching for John's bus, but it hadn't arrived yet, so I walked on the campus all by myself. While I was walking past the hallway, I saw a crowd standing in front of the notice board. There was no order, everyone was pushing and trying to get through. I ignored the scene and continued to my class which was on the first floor.

I've been studying in this school for more than five years, but it seemed weird to enter the class after a week. I was expecting a warm welcome from my fellows, but it didn't go that way. Everyone was busy with some strange activity. They were standing around Ted Hinton, laughing and celebrating. Some of them looked at me and waved, but the remaining smirked at me. I didn't like going near Ted's group as they were arrogant and mean, so I kept my cool and sat on the opposite side of the crowd.

I wasn't sure what was going on, but it wasn't bothering me, so I was fine with whatever was happening around me. While I was adjusting myself, Kim walked up to me and asked, "When did you apply for the captain position, you weren't here?"

"I-What?" I was shocked at first, but everything started making sense. I slowly and randomly walked out of the class, pretending as if I wasn't aware of anything. As I was away from everyone's sight, I ran downstairs to check the notice board.

I walked from within the crowd to the notice board, trying to get my sight over the list of captains. Mixed reviews were coming from different sides as I searched for my name. I scanned through, and my name was in last. I was leading Venus just like every other year.

I was always told that Ted, the captain of Jupiter, was better than me, but it was the time to prove myself and to prove my expertise. Our school arranges an inter-house captain competition of table tennis every year, but it was always Jupiter who secured the victory. All the houses had to kneel in front of Ted Hinton since his game was very professional. Just because of these victories, Ted and his group had become arrogant and mean.

I struggled my way out of the crowd and walked back to the class. I kept my emotions in-control as I didn't want anyone to consider me a weakling. Everyone was siding with Jupiter as they were commanded by the one and only Ted Hinton. While I was thinking intensively, the teacher entered and announced the schedule of the match. It was only two hours away.

By now, I knew that mom would have entered my name in the competition without letting me know, and she's the one who pushed me into taking the game training session. I wasn't scared at all as I believed in myself. It was time for me to show my skills and to embrace all the appreciation. I was sure that my three-month effort in the training session would be enough to secure victory against Jupiter.

However, there was still a sense of feeling and a sense of fear inside me, hiding somewhere that kept hold of my full potential. I walked to the washroom, looked at myself, and asked, "What are you scared off? I have to play as calmly as I played in sessions." I turned on the tap and splashed water on my face. "I can do it, and I can't let my efforts go in vain." The determination started revealing itself on my face. I was now fully prepared to face the opponent.

One after the other, Ted and I secured a place in the finals by defeating the other houses. While I waited for the finals under the shady tree, Ted came to me and discouraged me by reminding me of all my defeats in past. However, instead of feeling sad over it, I used it to fuel-up my determination. I was even stronger than before.

At the scheduled time, we were all gathering around the table. Everyone was supporting and cheering for Ted Hinton. Whereas, only a handful of people were showing their love for me. It didn't affect me as it was now a normal routine. I was used to it. Ted Hinton waved his racket in the air, smiling to his fans while I focused on the ping-pong in my hand.

The time had come, and the whistle blew. I swayed my racket and passed the ball over to Ted Hinton's court. The game's on! He wanted a slow start, so he gave a slight spin and paddled it back, but I wasn't in the mood to paddle away with the motion, so I smashed it back, leaving everyone shocked. That's a point for me! With every move he made, I had a counter-attack ready. Ted Hinton was shocked as he never saw me playing this strategically. I did lose some points, but I had a significant lead. Seven points for me, and four points for Ted.

The match continued and Ted's group started taunting me. It was the moment I felt a little degraded, I started losing points. I lost control over the game, and Ted came back in flying like a mighty soldier. The scores were equal, and there was only one point remaining. It was my turn to serve. All eyes were on me.

I looked at the ping-pong and out of nowhere, I remembered the instruction of my coach from the training session. He taught me 'The Ghost Serve' which was very difficult to learn. I wasn't sure if I was ready to use that serve here, but I had no other chance than to take this risk. I was sure that if I served it correctly, my opponent wouldn't be able to counter it. I took the risk and served. Luckily, the ball went right according to the way I wanted, and Ted was shocked as he missed the ping-pong.

"Point! Venus wins!" The referee announced.

I did it. Venus won, I won. I've never seen people so shocked in my entire life. Ted smiled at me, embarrassed, and I smiled back. I was at ease at last. It was the moment that changed my life and taught me many important lessons. I shook hands with my opponent and wished him luck for future competition. Now, everyone wants to be in with house Venus. Everyone wants to be like me, and it makes me proud. I believed in myself, and I did it.

NEVER DEVIATE

Tim, the only child of Mr. and Mrs. John, was born in a small town in North Carolina. He was just five years old when diagnosed with a memory disorder disease. Since both the parents were working, Tim remained under the supervision of his caretaker, Serene. She was instructed strictly to not leave him alone no matter what the situation.

Just like every other day, Tim woke up by the sound of the alarm. He rubbed his eyes, trying to look at the clock. Suddenly, out of nowhere, Tim had a severe headache. It was so intense that he covered his head with his hand and tightly clenched it. All of a sudden, the pain was gone, but so was the memory. Tim was lost. He looked here and there with complete confusion. He silently walked into the room, trying to figure out his present location.

Suddenly, Tim heard the footsteps of someone approaching his room. He quickly looked around the room, searching for a place to hide. He opened the door of the washroom and closed the door. To ensure his safety, he further hid behind the clothes of the wardrobe. Serene entered the room and noticed that Tim was not in bed. She walked over to the washroom's door and opened it. At this moment, Tim's heart was racing. He covered his head and ears with his hands and closed his eyes. Seeing the washroom empty, Serene got worried. She opened the door of the wardrobe and saw Tim hiding behind the clothes. "What are you doing here?" asked Serene.

Tim kept his eyes closed and didn't respond to Serene. Serene tried to convince Tim, but he wasn't responding. He stayed in the same state without moving an inch. Tim's attitude worried Serene, so without wasting any more time, she called his parents. She explained to them the entire situation, and his parents instructed Serene to stay near him until they arrive.

Tim was fighting with himself. Inside his unconscious mind, he was still there, but there was no possible way to find a link between the minds. He focused and focused, but with no result. Serene waited for his parents to arrive, and she was tired too of sitting, so she went to the kitchen to grab a cup of coffee. When Serene got back, Tim was lying in the wardrobe, fainted. The worried caretaker immediately placed her cup on the floor and pulled Tim out from the wardrobe. Since Tim was ten years old, it was difficult for her to pick him from the floor. She somehow managed to get him out of the washroom.

The worried caretaker hastily called the ambulance and informed them about the situation. In no time, the paramedics as well as his parents were at the door. Seeing the ambulance, his parents got worried and rushed inside to their son. The paramedic officer calmed the parents and told them to follow them to the nearby hospital without any delay. The parents nodded as instructed and brought Serene along to explain the entire situation to the doctor.

While the paramedics were trying to get back with Tim, there was a completely different war going on between Tim's mind. He was trying to fight off the disease. He walked along with his brain, watching the memories he had with his friends and family. Tim knew that if he lost hope, he will lose everything.

As they reached the hospital, the assistants took Tim to the emergency room and started preparing for procedures. The doctors were informed, and they arrived in no time. His entire case history was given to the doctors. They ran several tests, but all the tests were normal. Many different ways were tried to bring him back, but they failed. The doctors informed the parents that they are trying everything possible to get Tim back. However, they were unaware that he didn't want to go back unless fighting off the disease completely.

From the beginning, Tim was taught by his parents to never give up and to always complete the task at-hand rather than delaying it. As he walked down the road in his brain, a pathway of sorrow came across him. It was a dark, shallow route that seemed impossible to pass through. The entire road felt like quick-sand, pulling inside. It was the memories when his parents didn't have a job, and they lost their hope. They were unable to pay for his education, the bills, or the rent.

The entire journey to the unconscious mind was easy until this pathway appeared. Tim decided to wait for a moment and look back at the memories of his parents that were heart-clenching. Even though he was told by his parents to never look back on the past where the things were not in your favor, but he did. He didn't realize that these memories would ruin his determination and mission.

These memories seemed like depressed movie-clips that were projected by the brain. The surrounding darkness intensified the effects, and very soon, it started becoming obvious to Tim. Seeing his parents in stress and misery, Tim's eyes streamed with tears. The impact was so drastic that he didn't realize that he was losing himself.

On the other hand, the nurse immediately pressed the emergency bell which directly linked to the room of doctors. Within no time, the doctors rushed to the room. The parents got worried, seeing the situation. They motivated each other to stay strong, and maintain hope, as the doctors had encouraged. The medical staff checked the parameters and got worried as Tim's condition was deteriorating. After analyzing the monitors and reports, one of the doctors hasted to his parents and told them that Tim is in a coma. He further informed that they are trying their best, but it isn't clear if or when he'll wake up; it can be a minute, month, year, or maybe years. The doctor left, and the parents started crying.

After an hour, the doctors left the room in dismay and requested the parents to stay with their child as long as they can. The parents nodded and entered the room where their child was surrounded by different tubes and machines. Tim's father sat on the nearby chair while his mother sat beside him on the stretcher. They were helpless, and they could do nothing to change their child's condition. All they needed was patience and strength.

Suddenly, while they were grieving, an old lady entered the room. "Who are you?" the parents asked.

"I'm the oldest employee in this hospital," she said while walking over to Tim.

The parents nodded, but couldn't say anything. They watched the old woman staring at their child. "Is something wrong?" John asked trying to initiate a conversation.

The old woman nodded, staring at the child, and said, "My name is Anne, and I'm a psychiatrist in this hospital. Doctor Ibrahim asked me to give a visit to your child."

"Thank you so much, doctor Anne." Tim's mother said, keeping it formal. "You said that something isn't right with my child," John asked while getting off the chair. Dr. Anne nodded and said, "Do you know that your child can hear you speaking? Right now, he is fighting himself. I have seen many patients that have recovered from this condition because they were given hope from the outside. Your child is alone, and you are the only hope he has. I'd suggest that you get ahold of yourselves and start helping your child get out of the coma. I hope you understand what I'm trying to say."

The doctor's statement was a light in the darkness. It not only gave hope to the parents but also gave them motivation and determination. Anne checked the parameters and told his parents that she'd report to Dr. Ibrahim for some medications that will help him. The parents nodded, and the doctor left.

Even after an hour, Tim was stuck in the dark tunnel of miserable memories. It was as if he was lost in it. His conscious mind was becoming overwhelmed by the disease. He needed an external stimulation to push him back on track and that was to be provided by Mr. and Mrs. John.

After striving for two days straight, their voice finally reached Tim. It was like giving the soul back to the dead. With their voice, the miserable memories got shattered, and the dark pathway turned into daylight. It was the moment when Tim started walking again. When he took the first step, the parameters started showing progress which not only gave hope to his parents but also the doctors.

Everyone doubled their efforts, including Tim. In the next four days, Tim was back from the coma. His memory was back, and his disease had collapsed. He was just like every other normal child. With the motivation of the psychiatrist and the determination of Tim, parents, and doctors he was back with his parents. After a week of further testing and reports, Tim was discharged from the emergency ward to visiting wards.

NEVER JUDGE A BOOK BY ITS COVER

The sun was rising, and the birds chirping. The beautiful neighborhood radiated happiness, from Mrs. Johnson pacing about in the kitchen to Mr. Adam working on his car in the driveway. Every family in this neighborhood was connected. From sending each other food to having collective BBQs in Mr. Jack's backyard, everyone in this neighborhood liked each other. They were fond and had a great bond. The adults would spend the evenings talking to each other for hours while having coffee, and the kids would run around the street, making lots of noise. They all trusted each other so much that whenever Mrs. Johnson had to leave for her work trips, she would give Mrs. Adam a pair of keys. No one from this neighborhood had left in the past year, and no new neighbor had come, which was a significant reason for this close family-like bond.

Three of the naughtiest and the most loved kids from this neighborhood were always in the spotlight. Emelia, Noah, and Liam, all three were about the same age and had been friends for as long as they could remember. This group had done it all by running into the nearby forest to setting up firecrackers to scare adults. Due to how close everyone was, they were never reprimanded. It had given them such confidence that they were scared of no one in the neighborhood. But it was about to change quickly.

Today, the abandoned house, next to the park, was finally getting a family. All the kids were excited and hoping that the new family had kids so their gang could grow, and they could partake in more mischievous activities.

There were renovations on the abandoned house for about fifteen days. The kids got very excited every day, but no family would come. Today according to Noah's father, the family was coming. The excitement seeped out of the kids! Around Noon, the van had finally pulled into the driveway of the abandoned house. The kids had gathered around to see who the new family was. But to the dismay of the children, the family had not come with the moving company. When the kids inquired, the realtor told them that the new family would come in the evening. After a couple of hours of work, the moving company, under the realtor's supervision, moved everything and left. All the kids' excitement had faded, and they went back home.

By evening, everyone had forgotten what they were anticipating. They were all running around in the park when Liam saw a car pull in the driveway. Leaving everything, they ran, as fast as their little legs would carry them to the house. A stern-looking lady came out of the car, but no one else was there to be seen. Everyone wanted the car to have a lot of children, but only the strict looking lady greeted them. She had a lean figure and bony fingers. She always had her hair rolled in a bun and her mouth set in a straight line. All the kids thought she was mean and strict, so they knew they had to steer clear from her house. Disappointed, they went back to their homes.

Emelia went home to her mother and told her how everyone in the street was excited to meet the new family, but there's no one in that house except a mean-looking, lady. Emelia's mother corrected her right away and told her not to call someone mean just by judging how they look; that's not right. Emelia understood this, but looking at the lady made her so afraid that she did not want to go near that house. The conversation changed to her parents talking about meeting the new neighbor and welcoming them to the family. Even though Emelia did not want to meet her, she knew that she would be chastised right away if she protested. Her parents were very particular about respecting other people, and she had always been taught this while growing. This was why she did not protest when her mother said, "Tomorrow, Emelia and I will go over with cookies and welcome her."

The next day, Emelia, alongside her mother, found herself at the new neighbor's main door. The smell of the freshly baked cookies had spread across the street and was spreading happiness. The door creaked open. In the exchange that followed, Emelia learned that this new neighbor was named Meena, and she was alone. She recently moved to this town for her job. Emelia only cared about one thing: no new friends would be coming to this neighborhood. Meena invited them both inside and showered them with hospitality. But Emelia was sure this was all fake, and due to her mother's presence, in reality, she knew that Meena hated her and all the kids around. She was scared yet extremely bored, so she started looking around. The house was weirdly grim, shadowed due to the low lighting, and was empty. This all gave Emelia a bad vibe; she quickly ran back and sat down with her mother. After a little time, they finally said their goodbyes, and Emelia met with Noah and Liam. She narrated the story as she perceived it. In her report, Meena was extremely scary and dangerous. The kids continued to talk about similar things, how her porch was never lit, how there was never any sound coming out of her home, and how no one had seen her smile even once.

The group was convinced that there was something wrong. Even though Emelia was told not to judge someone based on their looks, Emelia did not want to risk getting scolded, so she decided to stay away from that house and not interact with Meena. Everyone in the group had a similar idea as they all had jumped on the bandwagon. A few weeks had passed, and no one had even talked to Meena once even though the adults had invited her over a few times. The parents tried to introduce the kids, but the kids knowing the reality, stayed away and did not interact. Emelia's mother had tried to explain how this was rude behavior, but her mind was made, and she decided to stick with the collective ruling that the group had passed.

Today was a mainly overcast day, but it was time for the kids to go out and play, and that is all they wanted to do. Without taking any precautions, the group had started to gather outside Noah's house to make their way to the park. Noah's mother reiterated how it was likely to rain, and the kids should not go. Disregarding all these cautions, the group marched down to the park and started playing around. The intense game of tag was about to finish when it started raining cats and dogs. The thunder rocked the neighborhood and scared every kid in the park. They found themselves seeking shelter under a shade in the corner of the park. They were stuck and very afraid. Noah wondered why he had not listened to his mother. Among all the chaos, Emelia saw that Meena was standing at the door gesturing the kids to come to her home.

Emelia looked at Noah and Liam. They all had the same thought; everyone was soaked and scared, but they were all afraid of Meena. Seeing that they have no other choice, everyone decided to run to Meena's house, who welcomed all the kids with hot cocoa and towels. At first, the kids were hesitant, but once Noah started using the towel, everyone got over their initial fears and dried themselves up.

It was still pouring, and Meena wanted to win the children's hearts and stepped up her game. She brought in snacks, put on an enjoyable movie, and pulled out a board game to play with the kids. Monopoly was on the table, and snacks were ready. This excited the kids. They spent the next few hours having a lot of fun. Once the rain stopped, the parents came to the park to find that no kid was in the garden, they looked around, but none of the neighbors had the kids at their home. This would have been worrisome, but Emelia's mother heard a lot of laughing from Meena's house. So, they found the kids quickly and safely.

As soon as Emelia got home, she started explaining everything to her mother. She told her how they were stuck and how Meena came to their rescue. She then confessed that she was utterly wrong to judge Meena as she did. She should have listened to her mother. Meena was too lovely, and they all had fun with her at her home. This changed the perspective they all had about Meena.

ALWAYS SPEAK THE TRUTH

As the bell rang, the hustle and bustle completely took over from the complete silence. The classroom suddenly was filled with various kinds of noises as the kids started packing up. One such kid was Jack. Introverted, he never spoke much, but he always had a clean academic record. Not very popular in class, but he was loved by his friends, which were few. His work was still a treat to mark for the teachers as it was mostly correct and entirely neat. Compared to what it took to check average work, Jack took half that time. Over the past few years, he had turned out to be a model kid with a spotless record. Jack also loved being in his mathematics class. He would eagerly go home and complete the given work. Even though Jack was good in all academic sense, his love for this subject made mathematics his most vital subject. Jack was always organized before everyone in the class, so he left the classroom early for recess. The hallway was empty.

Jack did not have a proper breakfast, and his stomach was growling. He paced past the hallway. At the turn, he could hear some rustling from the storage room. He was least interested as his head was entirely focused on today's lunch, but then he heard a sinister laugh, a laugh he recognized. It was his friend Jacob. He peeked inside the room to see that Jacob had a pair of scissors in one hand and what seemed like the shredded mascot costume in the other. The Eagle not only represented the school in various sporting competitions but was also the identity of the school. Jacob was the opposite of Jack. At times Jack's parents wondered how they were friends. Jack was the school's poster boy, without any issues with anyone, whereas Jacob was a magnet that attracted all the school trouble. Jacob had some part to play in all the pranks that were pulled on the premises. Whether it was blocking the door or ringing the bell, Jacob had done it all. Jack feared that Jacob had crossed a line as the students loved this mascot. "What have you done?" Jack said sternly but with a hint of worry. "HAHAHA! People will love this; I will be famous," replied Jacob.

"No, No one will love this; they will be outraged." Proclaimed Jack.

"Come on! Don't tell me you don't see the funny side of this?" said Jacob excitedly. What funny side, Jack thought to himself. Jacob continued to attack the mascot, and piece after piece kept falling to the ground. Jacob was having fun with this. "Can you stop, before we get in trouble?" pleaded Jack.

"You won't get in trouble; you're not even involved in this? If you're worried, why don't you leave?" replied Jacob. Even though he was scared, he could not leave a friend in this scenario. But before he completed his thought, the hallway was filled with thuds of footsteps. Before he knew what happened, Jacob was missing, and the History teacher had found Jack standing with shreds of the mascot and a pair of scissors at this feet. This would be hard to explain, he thought to himself.

Jack quietly followed the teacher to the empty teacher's lounge. He was ready to be chastised. But to his shock, the teacher was very calm and had some idea that Jack could not have done this task. All he wanted to know was the name of the student who did this. "So, I know, it not you. A few students saw someone run using the other door, and frankly, I know you are not the kind of the student who acts out like this. So please tell me who did this so we can move along and close the case. I would very much like to reprimand the student who pulled such an egregious task." The teacher explained in detail.

Jack, who knew that if he were to name Jacob here, he would be in trouble. Not only that, but his name was already maligned, and this might lead him to get expelled from the school. "I don't know who was in the room, I heard some rustling, so I went in to check, but by that time, that student had run away," Jack lied. "I refuse to believe this," the teacher replied, "You entered the room, and that is not enough to spook him to run suddenly; he must have seen you and vice versa. You're just trying to protect him.".

Jack knew he was digging a hole of lies, getting out of which might be problematic later. But he had no other way out, so he pleaded his case again, but the teacher did not accept. "If you do not confess, I will be forced to take you to the principal's office. Lying is not something this school tolerates.". Finding himself pinned in a corner, in his last hail mary attempt, he lied again but changed his statement in panic. "When I entered, there was no one in the room" he tried to get out, but his tongue slipped. It was too late now as the teacher caught him in his web of lies. He was taken straight to the principal's office, where his parents had also been called.

"So young lad, can you explain what this whole uproar is? We all know you didn't do it, but you're insisting that we punish you not only for this, but also for lying to your teacher?" Jack was so ashamed that he kept staring at the ground. He was in such a dilemma that he had no idea how he would get out. On one side, he had to protect his friend, or that friend might get in extreme trouble. On the other side, Jack was put on the chopping block himself. Jack had no idea what to do. Things worsened when his parents walked into the room. He could not even look up to see them enter. Fixed at a single point on the ground, Jack's stare was not moving. As the history teacher explained everything to Jack's parents, the tension in the room increased. Jack knew he had to convince his parents that he saw no one so that he could get out of this mess without anyone being hurt. But the conversation between the parents and the teacher was not coming to an end. "But I saw no one," Jack tried to interject, but the stare from the adults ensured that he did not interrupt them again.

Finally, after what seemed like an eternity, Jack was given a chance to defend himself. And like a broken record, Jack repeated, "I saw no one in that room." Everyone in the room knew that it was a lie. His father tried to explain the gravity of the situation, "Son! Look, if there was no one in the room and no one ran out, that means you are the one that shredded the mascot. Every clue points towards you. If you want to continue to save your friend, you can, but then you are the one who will have to face the consequences."

"Jack, I know you are being nice and are trying to protect someone, but if people don't face the penalties for their wrongdoing, they never learn. Today for such a harmless act, you might protect them, but what if tomorrow they do something that injures them or, worse, some bystander. We are proud that you want to help someone, but you should help people in a good way. If you continue this, the guilty person might never learn a lesson," continued his mother.

Jack's ambivalence still was not resolved. He did not want to see his friend get punished. "If I tell you his name, he will get punished. I do not want that; He is a nice kid who has issues with boundaries. I do not want to see him expelled," Jack finally expressed.

"I can assure you, this is not the worst prank that has been pulled in the long history of this school, the kid will not be expelled, but if he is not taught a lesson, then his next prank might get him expelled or even put in jail. Lying is never a solution."

Jack felt like he had no option. It would make life difficult for Jacob, but as Jack was told, it would also help make him a better person. If this is escalated and he is not stopped, he might end up in jail. Understanding that truth is always the right option, Jack decided to give in and tell his name. But before that, he ensured that the principal sticks to the promise of no expulsion.

See everyone deserves a chance. But you must remember that not everyone gets it. Jacob was lucky to have a friend like Jack, indeed.

THE LONELY LITTLE RABBIT

Liz loved pets, she loved animals of all kinds let it be rabbits, cats, dogs, birds, and even turtles. She loved them all. She thought they were so soft and she loved it when a stray cat would cuddle with her and purr. Animals were so sweet they took care of everything and dogs cheered you up so much! She loved it when a friend's dog would jump to her and attack her with kisses and hugs. It would light up anyone's day. Liz had always wanted a pet but she had never been able to get one as her elder brother Deke was allergic to dogs.

Deke was quite a bit older than Liz and had messy black hair that refused to lay flat on his head, an angled face with a pointy nose. He was about to start college away from home this year , so he was going to be moving out of the home. Liz on the other hand was a short girl with curly hair and freckles, her brown eyes twinkled like stars and shown like warm honey when under direct sunlight. Liz was about to turn six in a month and she was very excited as well, that was also going to be the day Deke caught his flight for UPENN.

Liz loved animals so much that she used to go to her friend Mike's house as he had a pet cat named Bells. She was a Persian white cat with a long, soft fur coat and blue eyes. She liked to sit in enclosed spaces and was friendly with only a limited amount of people. So when Bells would catwalk to Liz and purr beside her legs, Liz would take it as a compliment of the highest honor and lift the cat in her arms lovingly.

Liz had often asked her parents for a pet, but as time passed and Liz grew older even she understood that Deke could not handle a dog in the house. She made herself content with strays and pets of friends and family. Liz was quite resourceful when it came to solving problems like these, you see.

Sooner than the family had expected, Liz's birthday and Deke's departure arrived. The family had a small fancy brunch in which they had croissants, chocolate-covered strawberries, tea, fresh juice, and smoothies. They talked excitedly about Deke's college and Liz's birthday and how fast the children had grown up. Later they cut the chocolate cake, Liz's favorite, and set off to drop Deke at the airport.

"Happy Birthday again Liz darling!" Mom said on the way back from the airport. Mom was a plump little woman who always had the sweetest smile and gave the warmest hugs. She had almond-shaped eyes and a heart-shaped face. Liz thought her mother was lovely.

"So we have a surprise for you, love." Mom told Liz, her brown eyes shining. "A birthday surprise!"

"What is it Mum?" asked Liz excitedly, clapping her hands together with glee.

"Oh, you'll see, sweetie," Dad replied. "You will see when we get there."

It so happened that Mom and Dad took Liz to an adoption center, an animal adoption center to be exact. Liz could not be happier, she smiled so wide her jaw hurt, but she could not help it. She was going to have a pet finally! Liz kept hugging her parents to show them how special they had made her birthday.

"Now why don't you look around and choose a furry little friend to take home?" asked Mom

"I will!" Liz said her eyes shining in delight.

Liz circled the store and realized they had puppies, kittens, rabbits, and even turtles. They were all so friendly and they would purr

56

lovingly when you stroked their soft fur. All the animals were so healthy and energetic, Liz was in love.

But soon, Liz noticed a rabbit that was not hopping around like the rest of them. The store manager noticed Liz's interest and gently picked the rabbit out of his box and placed him on the table so Liz could see that something was wrong with the poor animal's leg.

"What is the matter with him?" Liz asked as she lightly stroked the rabbit's ears with her pointer finger.

"This little guy was born early, so one of his legs did not develop.

In the jungle, the rule of survival of the fittest is applied so the poor rabbit was left alone by his family." The attendant of the store explained. "Thankfully though some kind man found him and brought him to us. So, we took care of him, and now, he lives here."

"But he is so cute," Liz said sadly.

"I know, kid." The man said. "Why don't you guys make friends and I will go check on the other animals?"

"Okay," Liz agreed.

"Are you okay, little guy?" Liz asked the rabbit once the store attendant had left.

"No, I am sad." The rabbit replied.

"Why are you sad Mr. Rabbit?" Liz asked again, it felt normal to Liz that the rabbit could understand her she at times felt she understood them too.

"None of the rabbits play with me because I cannot hop as high or as fast as them. They make fun of me and I have no friends." The rabbit said sadly.

The rabbit was as white as the winter's snow, his fur glowed and he had black eyes so the contrast made his eyes look so mystical while the pink of his eyes and inside of paws made him look like a child's stuffed toy. Liz was in awe of his pretty features.

"And the humans do they take care of you?" Liz asked, concerned.

"The attendant feeds me and makes sure I am clean but no one ever adopts me. They only take home the healthy rabbits that can jump and play." The rabbit said. "So, I am almost always alone"

"But Mr. Rabbit you are so pretty, how can no one adopt you?" Liz asked as she was very confused. She did not understand why something like that would keep people from adopting the adorable little rabbit and he looked so sad! Liz wanted to help him.

"Because the rest of the rabbits are cute too, and they can also play, but I cannot play." He said

"Mr. Rabbit, do you have a name?" Liz asked as she now had an idea of how to help the poor rabbit.

"The attendant of this store calls me Snow, so I guess that would be my name." Snow replied.

"Mr. Snow, I am Liz, and I am very happy to meet you." Liz introduced herself holding out her fingers as a handshake.

"I am happy to meet you too, Liz," Snow replied, putting his front paw on Liz's outstretched fingers.

"Would you like to go home with me, Mr. Snow?" Liz asked.

The rabbit was overjoyed! He jumped as high as he could and it looked like he was doing the rabbit version of a happy dance. It was so adorable that Liz laughed out loud!

"I would love nothing more, Liz." Snow said after he had calmed down.

Liz smiled and took him in her arms and took him to meet her parents.

"Mom, Dad this is Snow and he is going to go home with us," Liz said.

"He is adorable!" Mom said. "I love his ears."

"Welcome to the family, Snow." Dad said as he hugged Liz "And happy birthday once more Liz."

"Thank you, Dad!" Liz said as she smiled. "This is the best birthday ever! I love you all and our new family member. I cannot wait to send Deke pictures!"

The three of them laughed and happily made their way home. On their way home, they bought their furry little friend a great many numbers of carrots and plenty of food. They roamed the alleys of the supermarket and picked out any of the toys that Mr. Snow leaned on. The family simply wanted to make their newest member happy and feel included. And with every new purchase, Liz simply felt like she was buying herself another present, so she truly could not have been happier!

Mr. Snow could not believe his fate. After years of patience and occasional sadness, he was finally going home with a family who truly loved him. He could not help but smile as he chewed on yet another carrot.

LIFE GOES ON

"James, can you please make me some mac and cheese today? I have a craving for some," Abby tugged at her brother's earphones to get his attention. James looked down at his five-year-old sister, pulling the earphones out of his ears and smoothing his curly hair.

"Mac and cheese, huh?" he asked, scratching himself under the chin.

"Yes, yes, please!" Abby wailed, making puppy dog eyes at her brother.

"Well I supposed that is a request I can cater to," he smiled, agreeing as he scooped Abby in his arms turning her upside down and tickling her before putting her back on solid ground, causing her to squeal, giggle, and kick around.

"You know, I think James is catering to the request of his belly more than yours, to be honest, Abby," Mum said, appearing out of her study unexpectedly.

"Don't blow my cover like that!" exclaimed James mock glaring at their mother.

"I knew it! He agreed way too soon Mum!" Abby snickered at her brother.

"See, your cover already was too shaky, you blew it yourself!" Mum laughed.

Abby laughed at her brother who looked cornered but then shook his head and smiled, showing the hint of white glinting teeth that proved he knew it was all fun and games. James was a tall lanky little fellow, who their mom said was too smart for his own good. He smiled at his Mum who winked back at him, hugging Abby.

You see, Abby and James had lost their father at a very young age. Abby had been only two. The wound was still fresh. But the three of them always came together to make each other laugh. Mum had quickly taken over the business and learned the tricks of the trade. There were days when Miss O'Conner worked from home when she did not have the strength to leave her kids behind, but rather wished to stay near them.

Those days she worked from home, hugging her children close, and just staying united.

Mum had a superpower, she could work in peace and chaos both, just as well. And boy, could she multitask. One minute she would be finalizing deals and then bent over millions of blueprints and multiple phone calls and conferences. And the next minute the same woman would be in the kitchen baking quiches and the best cheesecakes you had ever tasted.

When the calamity had hit them, Nana and Naani had offered to come to stay with them, help take care of the kids. They had already come over to help with the funeral preparations and had wished to make their stay permanent or at least extend it as they thought the new family of three needed their help and support.

Their father had been a firefighter. He was always the one who ran forward to help people. It was what he was made of, all he knew. He was always the first person you called when your car broke down in the middle of the highway, the first person you ran to when you had good news to share, and also the only person you'd wish to see when you just wish for a friendly face.

The children learned that from their father, to always help those around them. From their mum, they received the best advice or hints and nudges that pointed them in the right direction. James at times would laugh and say it was as if Mom got her inspiration from Hallmark cards or a daily fortune cookie and Mum would roll her eyes at him.

During the funeral preparations, the new family of three had been too in shock to process their surroundings. The children had lost their father due to excessive smoke accumulation in the lungs. There had been a fire in the City Hall caused by an unexpected gas leak. The firefighters had been at it for quite a while. Ensuring the safety of all congressmen and women had been a top priority and next was the extraction of files and paperwork that was crucial to the town.

Their Dad had helped out the Mayor and when she could catch a breath, she had huffed and puffed the location of a few critical documents that needed to be saved from turning into ash. And thus, being the man, their father had always been. He quickly nodded his head, set back inside, and into the heart of the fire.

However, Mr. O'Connor had also managed to make it out just in time. The minute after he had set his foot outside the burning building a loud and explosive, 'boom' had thrown all the nearby bystanders off their feet, into the air, and away from the fire. All the men had called Mr. O'Conner's a miracle or a narrow escape.

Little did they all know that just minutes later Mr. O'connor would be rushed to the hospital due to uncontrollable coughing, blockage in the throat, and stressed lungs. In a matter of minutes, Mr. O'Connor was no more. He had left behind two adorable children and a beautiful wife who now had to rethink their whole lives.

Thus, Nana had wanted to stay and help out in any way possible. She hated to see her daughter like this, the loss of a loving husband was great indeed. And while Mum appreciated the thought, she decided it wasn't the best decision for her or her kids.

Their mother was a strong resilient woman who believed with all her heart that if misfortune had struck you then good fortune must too. She also always believed that with your burdens came the strength to shoulder and carry them as well.

That was the sort of example she wanted to set for her children as well. She still called over Nana every time she wanted the extra hand or some moral support, or even just so she would be able to cuddle up next to her mom with a steaming cup of Nana's famous lemon and ginger tea. It was a concoction unlike any their mum had ever known and it always seemed to fill her up with energy.

On weekends Mum would either take them out for dinner or any place that the kids had had their eye on. On holidays when life felt the hardest and loneliest, Mum decided to take the whole family to either Nana's or their Dada's for the day. The good company and the close tenderness of family always managed to uplift the children's parents. They would either talk about all the fond memories they had of their father or share the sadness they felt because of how much they missed him.

It somehow always managed to do the trick. Always managed to make them all smile. Eventually, all of them learned that life, as they always say, goes on. And with time so do you. You learn to live with your losses and appreciate your joys.

So this year, when the anniversary of their father's funeral arrived. They decided they weren't going to shut down and cry behind closed doors. Mum decided that she wasn't going to close down. They were going to cherish the memories they had, and they were going to celebrate his memory instead of tarnishing it.

Thus the family of three got ready, they baked food; stuffed chicken and mashed potatoes, and also cake and muffins. They took all that food down to the fire department and shared the goodness, laughter, and smiles with the brave first responders.

Amidst the festivities, Mum noticed that James had wandered off to a corner. She excused herself and made a beeline for him.

"What's wrong?" she asked

"I miss him, Mum. And I don't like how much you have to do because he's not here," he whispered smiling sadly.

"James, my son. You are my strength. You and that little girl dancing around the firefighters. You two are all I need. I miss him too and I always will, but as long as I have you by my side, I know we will all be okay." she smiled at him, pulling him close.

"I wish I could do more," he said.

"James, you're the most helpful child I've ever seen. You help me cook and clean and you even make me tea without me asking for it. My child, it's okay. You just live your life and the rest will fall into place." she told him.

"I love you, mom," said James smiling at his mother.

"I love you, my son," she smiled back,

BOYS DON'T CRY!

Hectre and Kim were neighbors and classmates. Hectre was a slim lanky little boy with curly hair, and Kim was a pretty little girl with puffy, rosy cheeks and brown hair. They went to Wellington Primary Institution it was the best school in the neighborhood. The neighborhood itself was very beautiful. You could see beautiful flowers of yellow, pink, and white on the side of every road and pathway. They had a park in the neighborhood as well. The park had all sorts of swings and slides, of every color and style. It was fully green with grass and had a track around it for running, jogging, and walks.

Hectre and Kim were fast friends they were neighbors as well as class fellows. The two friends would always go to school together, Kim's mom would drop them at school in the morning, and Hectre's mom would pick them up when it was time to go home. Sometimes when they finished their homework early their parents would let them go to each other's homes to play together. On weekends or when the weather was nice, the families would go to the park. The two kids would play on the swings and the parents would make a picnic to eat and enjoy together.

Hectre and Kim would play all sorts of games together. Let it be cricket, dodgeball, or just your average running around or hide and seek. They would run around the whole school, laughing and playing and would have such fun.

This school year, the school hosted a bake sale. Kim brought home-baked cookies that her mom made, while Hectre brought homemade lasagne. Their mothers shared a stall and sold the food together. Both of the children helped as well. They would run all over campus deciding what they wanted from the other stalls. Kim bought herself an ice-cream and Hectre bought himself cake. After which they played ball together. It was a really good day for both of them.

Once when they were playing Hectre's arm got hit with the ball. It hit him very hard. He was very hurt. He started to cry, Kim rushed to him.

"Hectre! Are you all right?" she asked.

"I am hurt. The ball hurts very bad." cried Hectre.

Their teacher saw both of them and rushed towards them. She was a plump, short-heightened woman with curly brown hair. Somehow she always smelled of cookies and lavender. All the students loved her, she was always warm and friendly towards everyone.

"Hush now, Hectre." she said. "It is all right."

But, Hectre continued to cry as he was very hurt.

"Come on, Hectre, you know boys do not cry." explained their teacher.

"Why do boys not cry, teacher?" Kim asked as she had never heard anything like that before.

"Boys are strong, and Hectre is a very strong boy. Are you not, Hectre?" the teacher asked.

Hectre sniffled and wiped his eyes. He nodded.

"Yes, teacher, I am very strong." He said.

"Good boy, Hectre!" clapped their teacher.

And with that, the brave little boy swallowed back his pain and hurt. He was quiet in an instant. Yet, whenever Kim looked over and Hectre didn't know, she could see the poor boy's chin wobbling. It was obvious that the little boy was holding back tears! But he couldn't shed them as he was told that brave boys didn't cry. Thus he was going to take his hurt and simply bury it.

But then, the bell rang to announce break time, and all the kids ran to the sweets shop. Soon the ice cream and the chocolates made the two of them forget all about it.

It so happened that the next day Kim got hurt. They were running around when Kim slipped and tripped. She had a very bad fall and was very hurt. Kim started to cry. The teacher and Hectre both ran towards her.

"Are you okay, Kim?" they asked.

"No, I fell and I am in pain." Kim cried.

The teacher quickly covered Kim's leg and rubbed it to make her feel better.

"There, there now," she said. "It is all right."

Kim was still crying so the teacher decided to hug her. She opened her arms far and wide and took Kim in for a long warm hug.

"It is okay, little girl, you are okay. Just cry it all out." soothed the teacher. "I am here, Kim."

And Kim did. As soon as she calmed down, the teacher got her a glass of water and set her off.

Hectre's mother came to pick them up and took them home. Kim's mom was not home so she was invited for supper at Hectre's house. Both the kids had milk and cookies along with sandwiches; their favorite chicken and cheese! Once they were quite full they decided to take their cycles out and circle the house.

When they were walking out the door, Hectre accidentally stubbed his toe on the door which caused him to fall down a stair. Kim was behind him so she saw what had happened. She quickly offered him her hand and helped him stand up.

"Are you okay, Hectre?" she asked.

"Y-yes, I am," Hectre stammered.

It was very clear that the little boy was holding back tears but would not let himself cry.

"But, are you sure?" Kim asked

"Yes, I am fine." He repeated.

"If I had had a fall like that, I would have cried so hard," Kim replied.

"That is because you are a girl and girls are weak and they cry," said Hectre, standing up straight.

"I am not weak!" said Kim, angrily. She did not like being called weak. She was a big girl. "Look I can pick up this bicycle on my own! With one hand as well." And Kim really could, she held it up as high as she could even though her arms started to shake.

"Yes, you can pick up the bicycle, but you cry if you fall. So you are weak. I do not cry because I am a boy. And boys are not weak."

"But, that does not make any sense," Kim replied.

Hectre's mother heard their conversation and walked over to ask what the matter was.

"What are you two talking about?" Hectre's mother asked.

"Mom, boys do not cry because they are too strong, right?" asked Hectre in reply.

"Girls do not cry because they are weak! They are just as strong as boys!" Kim pitched in as well.

Hectre's mother looked at them confused.

"Who says boys do not cry, Hectre?" His mother asked.

"Our teacher told us." He replied.

Hectre's mother then sat them both down and explained. She told them that boys can cry. It is good to cry. Crying means you are hurt and that is all. Crying does not mean that you are weak. Even strong people cry; animals cry; men cry too. Girls do not cry because they are weak either. So they should never worry about being weak because crying does not mean you are weak. It only means that you are hurt. And anyone can get hurt.

Before we are boys and girls, we are humans. And the beautiful thing about being human is our emotions and our intelligence. They differentiate us from the rest. And to be able to express emotions is a gift, one that even the best of humans wish to possess. So whether we express our emotions, through tears or laughter. It is always a good thing to do so either way.

The children were listening intently to Hectre's mother when they saw Kim's car pull up. They quickly got up and smoothed their clothes.

"So now, you don't even have to hold back tears," smiled Kim at her friend.

"And, it's a wonderful thing to do!" Hectre agreed.

POWER OF CHOICES

Since childhood, Ken and Ben had been close. Some people believed that they were siblings just because of how they always hung out with each other. Ken was an energetic child who was ambitious and wanted to achieve a lot in life. His biggest goal was to represent his country in football. He always set high standards for himself, but this also meant that he was always pushing himself. Sometimes that would make him lash out in anger.

On the other hand, Ben was amiable, slim, and smart. His blue eyes complimented his blond hair. Unlike Ken, Ben was more focused on studies than he was on sports. This had caused issues between the two when Ken was inadvertently harsh on Ben while being hard on himself. Ben had always cared about Ken and understood the rationale so that he would let this slide. Ben was much more forgiving than he got credit for. He was just as ambitious as Ken, but Ken would always steal the spotlight due to the lack of energy he expressed. Ben did not mind that because he loved seeing his closest friend succeed in life. Things changed one day when Ben's school was playing a football match, against a rival school.

It was the semi-finals of the local school tournament. Last year, Ken's team lost in the final match, but Ken played so well throughout the championship that he was given the Most Valuable Player (MVP) award. Ken spent the last year training as hard as he could. He would be the first player on the ground and the last player to leave. He would spend hours on the training ground so that he could improve. It was not even related to just training; he kept a careful diet. He would spend more hours playing football than he would spend studying, but his parents understood his passion and supported him. As long as he got passing grades, his parents promised to take him to every training practice. This match was vital for Ken. By the 89th minute, it was close, and it looked like the game was going to end in favor of the rival school. Despite Ken trying his best, his team was not able to score. Ken kept thinking how if they had not conceded in the first 10 minutes, they would still have a chance to win. Right now, he just wanted to score an equalizer and move the game into over time. With the referee about to blow his whistle, Ken saw a chance when the deflected ball landed at the feet of Ben.

Ken sprinted past the opposing players and was in a prime position to tap the ball into the goal. Ben just had to cross the ball, and it was going to be alright. It was like time stopped for Ken, as he anticipated the ball coming in. He set himself upright in front of the goal, ready, just as Ben kicked the ball towards him. The ball gliding in the air, Ken realized that Ben had overshot the ball, and he tried to adjust the position so he could score, but the ball flew over his head just as the referee blew the whistle. Ken was extremely disappointed and stormed back into the locker room.

Players came in, changed, and left, but Ken did not have the energy to move. He was so angry that his team had lost but what infuriated him further was that none of the other players cared. His teammates came in, laughing and left without being worried. Finally, Ben came in looking for Ken. "There you are. I have been looking everywhere for you," Ben said, but Ken did not bother replying. Ben started worrying about his friend, so he sat down next to him. Ken exploded in anger, "Why did you not pass the ball properly; it was such an easy chance."

"I tried to, but..." Ben tried to explain, but he was interrupted by Ken closing his locker loudly. Ken started to march out of the door. Ben rushed and grabbed his hand. Before Ben could say a word, Ken jerked his hand out and pushed Ben away. Ben, struggling to regain his balance, found himself pinned against a locker. He was heartbroken. Ken had acted like this before as well, but this time Ben was hurt. He tried his best to get the ball to the right spot, but mistakes happen in the heat of the moment. It is not like the team did not have any other chance throughout the 90 minutes. Why was it that Ben was being blamed for everything? At this moment, he was so disgusted with his best friend that he did not want to ever see him again.

Ken, who was extremely angry, got home and went straight to bed without eating anything. His mother tried to convince him, but he was not going to listen. His parents found it best to wait until the anger had cooled down before trying to reason with him. Ben went home and seeing how sad he was, his father sat him down to talk to him. "Son, it was just a game! You tried your best, and it was just not meant to be," his father tried to console him. But it was not the match that bothered him. It was the actions of his closest friends that left him shocked. For a moment, he debated whether he should tell his father or not, but then he decided that he should take advice from his father. Ben always looked up to his father, so this would yield a good result for him. Ben explained how he tried his best to land the ball in the perfect place, but he could not, how Ken got angry, and all the things that ensued. Ben's voice cracked a few times, but he managed to keep himself from crying. After carefully listening to him, his father explained how what matters is that he tried his best, and it was not his fault that Ken reacted that way. If Ken does not treat him right, he should distance himself from such people. And Ben agreed with what his father said, he finally went to bed.

Ben and Ken were so close that they had always spent time together in school. They would arrive near each other, and until it was time to go home, they would be together. But today was different. Ben did not wait for Ken and had gone inside. When Ken entered the class, he saw that the seat next to Ben was already occupied. This made Ken sad, but he did not understand why Ben was acting this way. Ken felt that his actions were justified because he had worked so hard to get so far.

On the other hand, Ben felt very different and spent the whole day trying to avoid Ken; they did not even sit together to eat in the Cafeteria, which they had done every day since the 2nd grade. By the end of the day, Ken was desperate to talk to his friend and finally cornered him. When he tried to explain his part, Ben calmly replied, "that he was tired of getting treated unkindly, being angry does not justify his behavior, and if Ken cannot respect his best friend, then they cannot be friends any longer. It was time for Ken to look inside and see what was wrong."

Baffled and worried, Ken went home and decided to talk to his mother. He explained the whole story from the start of the game to what had happened at school. To his astonishment, His mother had also sided with Ben. She further reiterated the things that Ben had told him. Being angry does not justify mistreating someone. The person you are when you are mad is entirely under your control. It's your choice whether you want to give into anger and let anger rule you or stand up and prevent your loved ones from being hurt. She gave him an example that if mama bird got angry and yelled at the baby bird for doing nothing wrong, would that be justified? And Ken understood that his actions were wrong, and Ben meant to help him achieve his goals.

He had to see his friend right now, so he requested his mother to drive him to Ben's home, who obliged. When he finally saw Ben, Ken was embarrassed about how he had acted and apologized. He explained that he was entirely wrong to act like that and even apologized for the times in the past Ken had lashed out at Ben. Ben, who loved his best friend, quickly forgave him. Ben had realized that his friend now understood how he should act and felt it important to reward this behavior change. And with this, Ben and Ken got ever closer to each other.

FAMILY IS POWER

Jasmine was a marvelous girl who had always been energetic and ran around the house, helping her family. She radiated so much energy that her presence lit up the room. Her grandmother used to tell her stories that if she got sick and stopped laughing, everyone would be worried and sad, as if the sun had stopped shining. Jasmine extensively looked up to her grandmother, as she thought her grandmother was a fearless woman who, even though she lost her husband at a very young age, had managed to raise two amazing sons. One of them was Jasmine's father, John, who started his venture to support his family at the young age of eighteen. The business slowly grew and now had multiple branches all over the city. He was married to Sasha, one of the most academically gifted people Jasmine had ever met. Sasha got her Doctoral degree from a renowned university and was also teaching at that same university. The last member of Jasmine's family was her elder brother. Jasmine thought he was the coolest kid on the block, and Jasmine always wanted to spend time with him, but he was so busy. This was also true about her father and mother, who had work to do and could not make family time. But to fix this issue, they always had family time on the weekend to strengthen their familial bond. This was a big reason why Jasmine was so close to her grandmother and not as close to any other family members as they did not interact much during the weekdays. When Jasmine was young, this was not an issue, but as Jasmine started making friends and started relying on them, her family bond began to weaken.

Over the past few years, Jasmine did not have close friends who she relied on, but this year she started to hang out with a group of girls in her school. Emily, Mila, and Ella had been the popular girls of this school, and frankly, Jasmine had no idea why they had suddenly started hanging out more with her. But she needed some company, so she did not question this much and started hanging out. Emily was the daughter of a business tycoon and drove to school in her car. Mila's father was a politician, and that is all Jasmine knew about him. Ella's mother was the director of marketing in a multi-national company, and her father was on the board of directors of several companies. Jasmine felt really out of place when she hung out with them, but she did not think much about it and kept hanging out with them. Her parents had started noticing a little change in her behavior as well, she had started to flunk classes, and her quiz marks had dropped as well. Her mother wanted to talk about it, but she did not get the time to. "Let's go to the mall this Saturday," Mila suggested. Even though Jasmine knew that she had to be her family, but she agreed. 'I will be able to convince them,' she thought to herself.

That day Jasmine came home, and at the dinner table, she slightly mentioned that she might need to be dropped at the Mall on Saturday. Her idea was quickly shot down as they told her it was family time, and she could not get out of it. She pleaded, but that was to no avail. Angry, she went back to her room. 'I will still go,' she told herself.

Over the next few days, she tried to bring up the topic again, but she was quickly shot down every time she did it. They did not want to listen to any reason, and the reason for saying no was the family's norms. Every time she got angrier, and she spent the rest of the days sulking. Her grandmother knew what she wanted, but she flowered her with extra affection and lots of hugs as she could not give that to her. She even made good food for Jasmine over the next few days, but she could not get one smile out of Jasmine. This worried her, so she tried to talk to her son to let her daughter enjoy being a teenager. But her father, stubborn as always, refused to listen. But Jasmine was also determined to go, and she knew if her parents would not let her go, she had to sneak out. She planned that she would lie and go to Emily's house in the morning and turn her phone off and enjoy time at the mall. This was really out of character for Jasmine, so she was scared. She did not know what else she could do. This was for her freedom, and those people cared about her. Perhaps the most important reason was that Jasmine was afraid that she might not be included in any plans if she did not do what they wanted to do. Terrified, she went to her mother and tried to plead her case. But when she would not listen, Jasmine finally told her the biggest fear that she had. Her mother calmly replied that if you fear losing the friendship, you need to realize that you are not in a good company. "If your friends do not understand your responsibilities or limitations and force you to act against your comfort zone, then you should get out of those friendships," her mother elaborated further. It hit close to her heart, but she was not ready to believe that her friends were wrong. She quietly nodded and went back to her room to prepare for the stunt she had in mind for tomorrow mentally.

In the morning, she woke her dad up and explained how she needed to go to Emily's house for a project. She elaborated that she will be back in two to three hours. As she had always been a model child and her father cared about her academics, he did not think twice and agreed. Her heart was beating through her chest, and she tried her best to remain as calm as possible. Once in the car, the journey was quick and silent. As soon as she reached Emily's house, she told her dad goodbye and explained how she would call him as soon as she was free, and then he can come to pick her up. She went inside and met with Emily. They decided that they will leave for the mall in an hour. She was petrified, but once she got busy, it became easier for her. Just as they were about to sit in the car, she knew she had to make the last move. She texted her mother that she was going to the Mall with Emily and friends. After that, she turned her phone off. Even though she tried to change her focus on something else, she could not. 'It will be fine,' she thought to herself just as her gaze fell on the mall.

At the mall, they met with the entire group. They decided what Emily needed and would do that first. Emily chose a royal blue sundress and got a few accessories and shoes to go with it. She came out of the dressing room, dressed like a queen, she was looking stunning. Now Mila told them that they would get food. She asked Jasmine to reserve a table while the three girls went to place all the shopping bags in the car. Jasmine obliged and booked a table near the window, so they had a pretty view of the horizon. She waited for fifteen minutes but no one came. She got worried and went to look for them. She paced past the mall and into the parking lot but could not find them. The car was also missing. She was afraid and shocked. She took out her phone and turned it on. She tried calling Mila and Ella, but both did not pick up the phone. So, in a last-ditch effort, she called Emily, and just as soon as Emily picked up the phone, Jasmine realized she had been pranked. She could hear all three of them laughing at her. She was afraid and humiliated. She had no idea they planned on doing this. When asked why they did this, they had no reason. They just thought it would be funny.

It was not only humiliating for Jasmine, but she lied and fought to be there. She quickly ended that call and dialed her mother. Crying, she explained everything to her mother and requested her to pick her up from the mall. The mother consoled her and told her to stay put. While on the phone with her, she drove to the mall. Jasmine promised not to lie ever again, and her mother promised to make more time for Jasmine.

ACCEPTANCE

Finch was an adorable little kid. He had blonde hair, blue eyes, and a smile so bright, it would light up the room. Finch was an only child. He lived with his parents and went to a private primary school. He came from a very nice family. One which was very well off and well respected. Finch lived with his Mum, Dad, and their dog.

Their dog was a Goldendoodle, and they called him Dino. He was a very cuddly, funny little guy. Dino was the heart of the family. Everyone loved it when he would woof and run around. He would always get the morning mail and drop it in Dad's lap before he attacked him with cuddles and kisses. He would always play with Finch after he came home from school. The two of them would walk to the park and play fetch with the ball. On weekends, Mom would even prepare a picnic and the whole family would go to the park together. They would enjoy the yummy sandwiches that Mum made with tea and a good conversation. Mum would read a book and the boys would run around the park, playing ball and laughing. Finch was a happy little kid with a wonderful little family.

He loved Dino. They had both grown up together. Dino was Finch's pet brother and they loved to play together. Dino's bed was in Finch's room as well. The little dog would wake Finch up for school every day. It was the best way to wake up Finch. He would always wake up smiling because of his furry little friend.

One day when Finch went to school, he saw there was a new student in his class. The student was an immigrant. He and his family had just moved there from India and the little boy was on the brink of starting a new life in a new place.

The teacher introduced him to the class, his name was Aftab and everyone automatically started calling him Alex or even Alfred. Finch found the whole ordeal rather odd but then again the name Aftab, also sounded rather odd. So, he wasn't sure if he could blame his classmates for trying to make sense of such a foreign little sound. Not only that, the color of the newbie's skin was different too. It was darker somehow. It made Finch feel like the new child was dirty in a way he could not explain. Finch saw as the student made his way around the classroom and as he corrected everyone for mispronouncing his name, students made weird faces at him and dragged their chairs away from him. Inevitably, Aftab ended up sitting alone at the back of the classroom. He looked very sad.

Finch almost felt bad for him but he was also glad that he did not have to sit with Aftab either. The day passed and Finch saw Aftab sit alone in every class, and even during lunch, he quietly took out his lunch and ate in silence. While the rest of the students sat together, shared food talked, and laughed through the whole hour. Aftab almost looked used to it by the end of the day he did not bother correcting the students who did not use his correct name.

Although watching Aftab roam around alone made Finch feel a tad uneasy. He told himself it was because Aftab was a new kid. He remembered how he felt when he had been a new kid as well. It had been uncomfortable and Finch hadn't had any interaction his first few days either. But even despite all that, today, Finch was one of the most popular students in school. He was friends with everyone and even the seniors respected and were friends with him. So in due process, Aftab should be fine too. Everyone went through it.

"Didn't they?"

Finch came home that day and as per routine, Dino jumped on him in greeting making Finch laugh out loud. Finch told his mother about the new student in his class. Mum looked quite concerned although Finch could not figure out why. And soon he had forgotten all about it. The sight of chicken chili fries would do that to a child. And he ran off to gobble some down his throat.

Mum on the other hand was worried. Finch's reaction to the new student had concerned her greatly. She wanted her son to grow up to be a gentle and accepting little man, who was kind and friendly towards everyone, regardless of their color or appearance. She knew it was very wrong of her son to treat Aftab as he did. But she was also very careful about how she was going to handle the matter. She was well aware of the fact that she had to deal with this matter with great care as she realized that it was a very sensitive predicament. Thus she decided that she was going to talk it through with Finch's father and they would both find a way, best fit, to make Finch understand why what he did was wrong.

That weekend, the family went to the park-like usual. It so happened that Finch's neighbor and friend passed by. His friend's name was Damon. Damon also had a dog that he usually brought to the park to play and walk with. His dog's name was Milo he was bigger and fluffier than Dino. Today, Damon and Milo were accompanied by a new dog. Oh, how exciting.

"Damon, Damon, who is this? Is this yours?" jumped Finch up and down excitedly.

"Yes! I adopted a new dog," replied Damon. "Meet Tim!"

Tim woofed and jumped up and down in greeting. Finch was overjoyed as he loved dogs.

"Hi, Tim, I love you!" said Finch, happily hugging the little dog and petting his fluffy fur. The pup in return wagged his tail excitedly and licked Finch's toes, causing him to giggle.

They spent the evening playing fetch and having a laugh with all three dogs. Finch was filled with joy. He could not stop smiling. He took Damon and his dogs to meet Finch's parents. They were so happy to meet the new addition to the family. After the exchange of greetings, welcoming the new member, and one too many congratulations. Everyone sat and enjoyed the hearty picnic food that Finch's family was famous for.

When Damon left, Finch ran to his parents and started jumping up and down.

"What is the matter, Finch?" asked Mum laughing, at his little son's antics.

"Mum, Mum, I want another dog!" said Finch.

"But, you already have a dog!" replied Mum, mocking her surprise when she had seen that request coming the second she had met Damon's new dog.

"But Mum, I want more!" said Finch excitedly. "I want a dog in every size, color, and shape. Mum, please!"

Those words instantly gave Mum a brilliant idea. Clever little Mum calmed Finch down and told him they had to have a conversation with him. She even gestured to his father, who quickly realized what was going on and caught up to speed. All of them sat down on the soft blanket. The grass underneath their feet was soft and moist, it felt very calming.

"So, remember how you just said you want a dog in every size and color, sweetie?" asked Mum, repeating her son's words back at him.

"Yes, Mum," replied Finch, curious.

"So, just like there are dogs of every lineage and every color, so are humans, my darling," said Mum.

"In your life, you are going to meet people who are white, brown, black, and everything in between. You are going to meet people who might have disabilities. Not everyone is as blessed as you are, sweetheart. And you are going to have to treat them just like you treat Damon, okay? It is not nice if you don't treat them the same. Think about it Finch would Tim like it if Damon only played with Milo and not him? It is not nice. We must be better than that."

Finch thought about it for a minute. Then he nodded, thinking hard. He could tell where his mother was coming from. He still recalled how bad he felt when he saw the way Aftab had been treated on his first day. New kid or old, no one deserved that.

"I understand, Mum," said Finch.

The next day when Finch went to school, he greeted Aftab properly with his correct name and sat next to him. Both of them talked, laughed, and soon became good friends. When it was time to go home, Finch invited Aftab to come to his house. Aftab agreed and they both went home together.

Finch's mom could not be happier or prouder of her son. She was so proud that all four of them went and adopted a new dog together. That is when Finch understood that everyone, no matter how different they may seem they still deserved to be respected, accepted, and loved.

And if no one around you was practicing it, then you must be the first one to do so.

Thank you for reading and using this book, you have already taken a step towards your relaxation

Best Wishes